Adapted by Alice Alfonsi
Based on the series created by
Michael Poryes
Susan Sherman
Part One is based on the teleplay written
by Dava Savel.
Part Two is based on the teleplay written
by Bob Keyes & Doug Keyes.

New York

Printed in the United States of America

First Edition
1 3 5 7 9 10 8 6 4 2

Library of Congress Control Number: 2004107696

ISBN 0-7868-4640-2

For more Disney Press fun, visit www.disneybooks.com
Visit DisneyChannel.com

Part One

Chapter One

School was over and the stampede was on.

Crowds of kids poured out the front doors of Bayside Junior High, making their break for freedom. Raven Baxter couldn't wait to join them.

"Oh, hey, Rae!" called Raven's best friend Chelsea Daniels from across the hall. "You want to come over and do that biology homework and rewrite that history paper?"

Homework? thought Raven, slamming her locker door shut. My girl needs a reality check. When school is done, you got to bring on the *fun*!

"I'm sorry," said Raven. "I didn't quite catch that."

Chelsea got the message. "You want to go shopping and get a pedicure?"

Raven grinned. "That's what I *thought* you said."

Suddenly, Raven froze. Every molecule of her body seemed to tingle, and time seemed to stop.

Through her eye
The vision runs
Flash of future
Here it comes—

I see my parents standing by the front door of my house, and—uh-oh, not good—they don't look happy.

Now they're opening their mouths. They're about to say something—

"No, no, and no!"

The vision ended as abruptly as it began. Raven blinked and said, "That was weird. I just had a vision of my parents saying 'no!'"

"About what?" asked Chelsea.

"Hello? They're parents," said Raven. "Do they *need* a reason?"

Just then, Raven noticed a good-looking older boy striding down the hallway. At the end of the corridor, he stopped and began to look around.

"Chelsea," she whispered, "look, there's that cute guy from the video store."

Chelsea checked him out. He had broad shoulders and was holding a set of car keys. "Wait, he's in high school," she whispered to Raven. "What's he doing here?"

"I don't know, but teeth check!" cried Raven.

The "teeth check" was a move the girls had come up with back in grade school—the day after Raven had delivered a book report to her entire class with a piece of spinach stuck between her two front teeth.

Both Raven and Chelsea bared their teeth, and gave each other the once-over.

"You're good," the two said together.

Now for phase two of our "meet the cute guy" routine, thought Raven.

"Ha-ha-ha!" laughed Chelsea.

"Ha-ha-ha!" Raven laughed back.

They glanced in the cute boy's direction. He hadn't noticed them. Dang, thought Raven. She shot a look at Chelsea, and the two girls moved closer to him.

"Ha-ha-HA-HA!" laughed Chelsea, even louder.

"Ha-ha-HA-HA!" echoed Raven, louder still.

Okay, thought Raven, do *not* tell me you can't hear me *now*!

"Hey, Raven!" called the boy when he finally glanced over.

"You know my name?" Raven asked, genuinely surprised.

"Yeah," said the boy, "you rented *She's All That* about two weeks ago. I sent you the late notice."

"The one with the smiley face?" asked Raven.

"Yeah, that was me. My name is Matthew," he said, holding out his hand.

Raven smiled as she took Matthew's hand. It was warm and strong—and when he smiled back at her, every muscle in her body seemed to melt.

"So, um, I'm here to pick up my little sister," said Matthew. "Why are you here?"

"I'm here—" Raven was about to say, "because this is Bayside Junior High, and I, like, *go to school* here." But just in time, she stopped herself.

Obviously, Matthew thought she was in high school. And Raven wanted him to *keep* thinking that.

"I'm here, I'm here . . ." repeated Raven, thinking fast. "You know, to pick up my little brother, Eddie." She pointed to her other best friend Eddie Thomas, who had just walked by.

"Eddie!" she called, shaking her finger at him. "Mom told me to give you a bath before dinner."

"Say what?" asked Eddie.

Raven quickly turned to Chelsea. "You go make sure he doesn't wander off."

Chelsea nodded, racing up to Eddie and ushering him away before he could blow Raven's cover.

"So, Raven, I know we just sort of met," said Matthew, flashing his killer smile again, "but would you like to do something with me Friday night around eight?"

Raven hesitated. All the magazines said you should never accept a last-minute date with a guy.

"Wait. I don't know, Matthew," said Raven. "It's kind of short notice."

She had to show Matthew that she was a girl who made dates on her own terms. She wasn't desperate—no way, not Raven Baxter.

"Eight-*fifteen*?" she quickly suggested.

Matthew agreed, and after they said good-bye, Raven rushed off to find Chelsea.

"I have a date Friday night!" squealed Raven when she met up with her friend. "And he's seventeen."

Chelsea shook her head. She hated to burst her best friend's bliss bubble, but she knew how strict Mr. and Mrs. Baxter were.

"Rae, your parents are not going to let you go out with a seventeen-year-old—" Chelsea stopped as she realized something. "Wait, Rae, that's your vision. Your parents are going to say, 'no.'"

"No, no, no," said Raven. "See, that's only the first 'no.' The trick is you keep asking, asking, and asking—"

Later that afternoon, Raven did keep asking, and asking, and asking if she could go out on a date Friday night.

Her parents were about to leave the house. But Raven was sure if she just kept hammering, she could pound that stubborn parental wall to dust.

Their final answer came before they left: "No, no, and no!"

Raven was stunned. Not only had they refused to budge, they had even turned her down *in unison*, just like her vision.

"But can't we even talk about it—?" Raven complained.

Slam!

The door shut right in her face.

A moment later, her dad cracked the door and sheepishly peeked back through.

"I'm sorry, that was rude," he said. "Where was I again? Oh, yeah. *No!*"

This time the door shut for good.

Chapter Two

"**I** can't believe they just walked out," said Raven, pacing the floor of her bedroom an hour later. "I mean, they never listen to anything I say."

Raven turned to Chelsea, who was sitting on the bed. "Do your parents listen to you?"

"Well, they kind of have to, Rae," said Chelsea with a shrug. "They're both therapists. It's just a little weird when they say my time's up and they'll see me next week."

Raven sighed.

"Rae, you have to call him and tell him you can't go," said Chelsea, placing the phone in Raven's hand.

"I can't do it. You do it," said Raven, holding

the phone out to Chelsea. A second later, Raven pulled the phone back. "No, I'll do it."

Then Raven changed her mind again and again and again—"No, you do it. No, I should do it. You do it."

The phone flew back and forth so many times, Chelsea was beginning to feel dizzy.

"Raven!" she cried.

"Fine," snapped Raven, copping an attitude. "If you don't want to do it, just say so." She took a deep breath, strolled away from Chelsea, dialed Matthew's number, and waited for him to answer.

"Hello, Matthew," Raven said in a voice perkier than a cheerleader's. "It's me . . . *Chelsea*, Raven's friend."

Across the room, Chelsea's jaw dropped. She raced over to Raven and tried to pull the phone away—with no success.

Raven just kept on talking in her high-pitched "Chelsea" voice. "She told me to *call* you to *tell* you that she *so* can't make it Friday night—"

Suddenly, Raven froze.

Through her eye
The vision runs
Flash of future
Here it comes—

I see my parents standing by the front door of our house again—but this time they're all dressed up, like they're going dancing.

Now Dad's spinning Mom around and finishing the move with his signature dip.

Awright! They ARE going dancing!

The instant Raven came out of her vision, she

knew exactly how to end her phone conversation with Matthew—

"But she'll be able to make it *Saturday* night," said Raven, still using the cheery "Chelsea" voice. "Oh, yeah. And let me *just* tell you, you are, like, *so* lucky, because she had *so* many offers that night. So you two lovebirds have a *good* time. All right, *bye.*"

As Raven hung up, Chelsea stared at her in disbelief. Hands on hips, she said, "Okay, first of all, I *so* don't talk that way—"

Chelsea frowned when she listened to her own voice—and realized she actually *did* sort of talk that way. Sighing with frustration, she added, "And *hello*, your parents said you can't go!"

"Actually, I just had a vision that my parents were dancing in the living room," Raven explained. "And there's only one night when they go dancing: Saturday. It's perfect. They'll never know."

"Okay, let me make it, like, so un-perfect. When you're on your date, who's going to babysit Cory?" Chelsea asked.

For a moment, Raven frowned. Then she gave Chelsea one of those sly smiles that said, "Hey, girl, isn't that what friends are for?"

On Saturday night, Chelsea arrived at the Baxter house dreading her secret babysitting duty.

Raven's little brother, Cory, was a cute kid, but his annoying Mr. Slick Ladies' Man routine was wearing Chelsea out.

She had just started doing her homework on the Baxter's living room couch when the nine-year-old came swaggering out of the kitchen, a bowl of popcorn in one hand, breath spray in the other.

"Our first night together, baby," said Cory with a wink. Then he spritzed the spray into his mouth, sat on the couch next to Chelsea, and put his hand on her leg.

Chelsea didn't let it bother her. She just took the bowl of popcorn—and dumped it on Cory's head.

Just then, Mr. Baxter burst through the kitchen door, humming a dance tune and trying out some moves across the living room floor.

Chelsea and Cory turned around on the couch to watch. A little James Brown, a little Gene Kelly, and some moonwalking to top it off.

"The man's good," said Mr. Baxter with a smile.

"But he's nothing without his baby," came Mrs. Baxter's voice from the top of the stairs.

Raven's mom sashayed down the steps as if moving to a spicy salsa rhythm. When she reached the bottom, Raven's dad twirled her around and around.

Raven walked into the living room with a big smile. "You clean up pretty good," she told her dad. He was wearing a pair of dark blue dress pants and a matching vest over a lavender dress shirt.

"Well, thank you very much," he replied. "Now say something nice about your mother."

"Mom, you look hot," said Raven. And she really did. Mrs. Baxter's bright red dress had a trim bodice and a flowing skirt perfect for dancing. And her matching red shawl looked really elegant draped over her bare shoulders.

Mrs. Baxter turned to her husband. "See? I got a 'hot,'" she said smugly. "You just got a 'pretty good.'"

"Well, that's because she didn't see me do this." Raven's dad twirled her mom around and finished with his famous "jiggy down" dip—just like Raven's vision.

"Now that's hot," said Mr. Baxter.

"No, that's painful," said Mrs. Baxter, rubbing her neck.

"That's because I need to do my thing on the dance floor," said Mr. Baxter. "I can't get my jiggy down with a couch here."

"Well, let's not waste any 'jiggy down' time, okay?" said Raven, holding the door open for them.

Her parents smiled at her. Dressed in a thick terry cloth robe and shower cap, Raven looked as if she was ready for nothing more than an evening of home beauty treatments—which was just fine with them.

Mr. Baxter decided his daughter was right. Why waste any time? Grabbing his wife's hand, he began twirling her right out the front door.

"Wait a second," said Mrs. Baxter, turning to Raven. "Any problems, you call me on my cell—"

But Mr. Baxter just kept twirling her.

"Now, Victor, I see what you're doing," complained Mrs. Baxter, "and if you think you're just going to rush me out that door—"

But it was too late. She was out!

"And I want that popcorn cleaned up—" Raven's mother called over her shoulder before Mr. Baxter slammed the door shut.

A second later, the door opened again. "Like I said," bragged Mr. Baxter, "the man is good."

When the door shut again, Raven turned to face Chelsea and Cory. "They're going out," she told them, "and so am I. Check it out."

Raven pulled off her shower cap and her sleek black hair cascaded down to her shoulders. A lovely white flower was clipped to one side.

Next, she untied her terry cloth robe, let it drop to the floor, and struck a pose. She'd put together a slammin' outfit for the evening—

silver sandals, a long, ice-blue satin skirt with a silver belt, and a sparkly baby-blue sweater. She wore dangling white earrings and a glittery silver necklace and bracelet set that matched her belt perfectly.

Over it all, she wore a lightweight navy jacket. "It's my own creation," she said, showing the jacket off proudly. "Looks like a jacket, works like a purse."

She opened the jacket wide to reveal a half dozen little pockets she'd sewn up and down the lining, each one holding a different item.

"I got . . . the cell phone, the lip gloss, the nail file, and an extra dinner roll, just in case, you know, I don't like the food at the restaurant," she told them.

"Rae, you look gorgeous," said Chelsea.

Cory might have complimented his sister, too, if he hadn't been completely obsessed with his babysitter.

"You want to see gorgeous, baby?" Cory asked Chelsea.

Before she could say, "Definitely not!" Raven's little brother whipped off his sweat-suit jacket and struck a pose like a body-builder.

Chelsea tried not to laugh at Cory's little white tank top and big gold medallion. She knew he was trying to come off like a hip-hop version of Mr. Universe, but the nine-year-old looked more like Winnie the Pooh.

"I know," said Cory with a Mr. Slick wink, "like a dream come true." But when the kid leaned toward Chelsea for a kiss, a strong hand suddenly yanked him back.

Eddie Thomas had come in through the back door and was now pushing Cory aside to sit next to Chelsea himself.

"Back away, sham," Eddie advised.

Cory was horrified. "What's *he* doing here?"

he asked Chelsea. But it was Eddie who answered.

"Well, *I'll* be your date for this evening," he told the lovesick little boy. Then he winked. "Like a dream come true, ain't it sugar?"

Chapter Three

Later that evening, Raven felt starry-eyed. This was not only her first date with a high-school boy, it was her first *car* date, meaning her date was actually the one *driving* the car— not his brother, not his father, not his grand-mother, but *him*.

"So, you drive a car. Oh, that is so cool," she couldn't help gushing as they sat down at a table for two at a romantic Greek restaurant.

Matthew looked at her in confusion. "Don't you drive?"

Raven's smile froze in place. She was *sup-posed* to be acting like she was older than four-teen. So she quickly added, "Yeah, but you know, *your* car has that *new*-car smell."

Uh-oh, thought Raven, as soon as she saw the reaction on Matthew's face. This might have been a Greek restaurant—but her date wasn't supposed to be looking at her as if she had just *spoken* Greek.

"Well," he said, "the car was my *grandfather's*."

"Oh, you know me," said Raven with an awkward laugh. "I love the new-car smell. *And* the old-people smell. Love 'em both."

Meanwhile, back at the Baxter house, Eddie was wondering what Cory was up to with the vacuum cleaner. He didn't trust the little hound dog—not for one second.

"Hey, man, what'cha doing with that?" Eddie asked, eyeing the vacuum suspiciously.

"Cleaning up the popcorn," Cory said as he pushed the machine into the living room. Then he shook his head dejectedly and said,

"Who am I fooling, thinking Chelsea would ever like a stupid little kid like me?"

Eddie's heart melted. The kid sounded really shattered. With his head hanging down he looked more like a wounded puppy than a super-slick hound dog.

"Oh, man, look, just give it some time," said Eddie, putting his arm around Cory's small shoulders. "In five years, you'll be fourteen. And of course, Chelsea will be nineteen, and she still won't be looking your way. . . . Good news is, I'll be dating college girls."

"I'm just impressed you got the math right," said Cory with a smirk. Then he reached down, opened up the vacuum, and innocently asked, "Could you help me with this vacuum bag? It's a little full."

In the next room, the phone rang.

"Hello?" said Chelsea, picking up the cordless

receiver on the kitchen counter. "Oh, hi, Rae."

Raven was talking on the other end of the line, but Chelsea didn't hear her. The roar of the vacuum had started up in the living room. Then Eddie began yelling, "You are so dead meat!"

"Uh-oh, hold on," Chelsea told Raven.

With the receiver in her hand, Chelsea ran into the living room. She found Eddie still hollering, and for a good reason. He was completely covered with vacuum-cleaner–bag dust—and Cory was holding the bag.

"Maybe you should go home and take a shower," Cory sweetly suggested to Eddie.

"Forget it," snapped Eddie. "I'm taking a shower right here!" Furiously, he climbed the staircase. "'Help me, Eddie, the bag is full!'" he said, mimicking Cory in a whiny little-boy voice. "You little Oompa Loompa!"

Cory snickered and turned to Chelsea—

Oh-no, she thought, Mr. Slick is back!

Pulling out his breath spray, Cory spritzed his mouth, then headed for Chelsea with his lips puckered.

Chelsea did her best to stiff-arm the charging kid, her hand firmly planted on his little forehead. But she didn't know how long she could keep it up!

"Raven, when are you coming home?" she cried into the phone.

"Pretty soon if I keep messing up on this date," said Raven.

After she and Matthew had ordered their food, Raven had left the table to visit the restroom. Now she was standing outside the women's room, talking on her cell in an attempt to regain some confidence.

"He is so mature," she told Chelsea, "and I'm acting like such an idiot. You should have heard the lame things I said about his car. He's going to figure out I'm not seventeen."

"Look, Rae, just be honest with him and tell him your real age," advised Chelsea. "He's a nice guy, I'm sure he'll understand."

Raven rolled her eyes. "You don't get out much, do you?"

"Look, Rae," Chelsea tried again, still holding off the lovesick Oompa Loompa, "just let him do all the talking. You just . . . you just . . . you just sit there and . . . look *old*!"

After Raven rejoined her date, she decided she wasn't just going to look old—she was going to *sound* old, too.

"So, *do* tell me about your life," Raven purred in a deep voice as they ate their appetizers.

"You gonna finish that?" asked Matthew, pointing at her plate.

That wasn't the reaction Raven had expected. "Uh, I was going to put it—"

Before Raven could finish her sentence, Matthew snatched a big piece of calamari from her plate.

"Okay, well, you can take it," said Raven, since he already had.

"Hey, I do love calamari!" he told her. "You know, calamari is just a fancy name for squid."

Matthew took the squirmy piece of seafood and waved it in front of Raven's nose. "Oh, look!" he teased in a high feminine voice. "Save me from the squid, Matthew. He's big. He's trying to get me, Matthew!"

Raven stared at her date—what was up with *this*?

"I'll save you, baby," he finally said in a deep, macho voice. Then he popped the piece of calamari into his mouth and began to chew.

Okay, Raven told herself, so Matthew has a weird sense of humor. So what, right?

A few minutes later, the waiter served their soup, and Raven watched in horror as Matthew began hastily spooning the stuff into his mouth like a toddler at feeding time. The creamy soup coated his lips and dribbled down his chin.

"Well, let's see," he said, spewing the soup as he spoke. "I was born in San Francisco. My father's name is Jerome, he's an optometrist—"

On the last word, Matthew sprayed a mouthful of soup all the way across the table and into Raven's face. And the worst part was, he didn't even notice. He just kept shoving the spoon into his bowl then back into his mouth.

Raven could not figure out why her hot seventeen-year-old date was acting so immature. She closed her eyes, took a deep breath, and prayed the next course would *not* involve liquid.

When the main course came, Raven was relieved—lamb kabobs and rice seemed totally slob proof. How difficult could it be to eat a kabob? she asked herself.

But Matthew found a way.

First, he began gnawing the meat off the stick in the sloppiest way possible, smearing grease all over his cheeks, chin, and fingers. Then, he started chewing with his mouth open.

Finally, as he yammered on about himself nonstop, he spewed bits of meat all over the table. ". . . and when I was seven," he said, between open-mouthed chews and sprays of meat scraps, "I tried going to this camp in the woods . . . but you know . . . it was the whole wilderness thing, you know—"

Just then, a large meat bit flew across the table and plunked right into Raven's glass of soda. Eww, gross! she thought.

Matthew never stopped talking. He just reached over, shoved his greasy fingers into her glass, retrieved the half-eaten piece of meat, and popped it back into his mouth!

"Way too prehistoric for a brother," he continued.

Right, thought Raven. *Prehistoric* was definitely the word.

By the end of the main course, Raven didn't think her date could do anything to gross her out any more than he already had. But once again, Matthew managed to surprise her.

Telling her he wanted to give her something special, he pulled the napkin off his lap and began folding it into a triangle. Then he leaned forward, and before Raven could stop him, he slapped the dirty, greasy "napkin hat" onto her head!

"You wanna see what I can do with a table-cloth?" he asked.

"No!" Raven said immediately.

Finally, with a defeated sigh, Raven had to admit to herself that this date was a disaster.

Carefully, she pulled the napkin hat off the sleek hairstyle she'd spent hours working on and said, "Matthew, I really hate to see this . . . this . . . *wonderful* evening end, but, um, I'm really kind of sick. Could you take me home?"

"Uh, yeah, sure," said Matthew, looking a little surprised. "Let me just get the check."

"Waiter? Waiter?" he called politely.

None of the busy waiters seemed to notice. But Raven definitely needed this horror movie to end—*now*.

"Waiter!" she yelled at the top of her lungs. *Crash!*

She had startled so many members of the restaurant staff, one of them dropped a huge tray of silverware.

As Raven turned to see what all the fuss was about, she saw a sight that made her gasp. At the entrance to the main dining room stood a handsomely dressed couple—Victor and Tanya Baxter!

Quickly, Raven sank down in her seat. What were her *parents* doing at this restaurant? Raven wondered. She thought they had gone dancing.

As the maitre d' showed her mom and dad to their table, Raven overheard the answer.

"I can't believe I split my pants wide open," Mr. Baxter was saying to his wife as they walked through the dining room. "Just when I was getting my jiggy down."

Raven noticed that the red shawl her mother had draped elegantly across her shoulders earlier that evening was now tied *in*elegantly around the seat of Mr. Baxter's pants.

"And you're going to *keep* your jiggy down," Mrs. Baxter told her husband when they reached their table. "Sit."

Still slumped down in her own seat, Raven tried not to panic. Her parents were sitting at a table with a clear view of the restaurant's front door. If she walked out now, they'd definitely catch her.

"Change of plans," she told Matthew quickly when she saw him rise to leave. "Sit. We're staying."

"But I thought you felt sick," he said.

"Sick. Yes, I do. Yes," she said.

And it was true. She was sick at the thought of her parents seeing her out on this date!

But to Matthew she said, "I'm sick at the thought of ever letting this date end."

Just then, Raven's father walked right by

their table. In a panic, Raven dumped the bread basket and held it in front of her face.

"Oh, look," she told Matthew. "I'm a hockey goalie!"

"Cool!" said Matthew, grabbing a roll. "Goes left. Goes right." He shot the roll at the basket. "Score! Yeah, who's the man?"

Underneath the basket, Raven rolled her eyes. She had just figured something out. Seventeen-year-old Matthew had the very same sense of humor as her little brother, Cory.

Scratch that, thought Raven, when she felt a second roll hit her bread-basket face mask. Actually, her nine-year-old brother acted way more mature.

Chapter Four

"**O**pa!" cried the restaurant's waiters.

Uh-oh, thought Raven. She had seen that movie about a Greek wedding, and she knew what "Opa!" meant—Greek *dancing*!

Greek music flowed through the sound system, and the waiters started clapping their hands as they walked from table to table, encouraging some of the female patrons to get up and join them in a circle dance.

"Opa!" cried Matthew, clapping his hands.

Raven sank down even more in her chair. "Opa," she muttered. "Whateva."

Suddenly, Raven heard footsteps coming toward her. A pair of waiters waved at her to get up.

"No, I don't dance," she told them, trying to slump further down in her seat. But they pulled the table away!

"No, I'm too short. I'm too short!" she cried.

But it was too late. "Uh, thank you, all right," she said—what else could she say? They were already picking her up and sweeping her across the dance floor!

Luckily, Raven's parents were too busy arguing to notice their daughter was heading right for them.

"Come on," Mr. Baxter told his wife. "I want to get my 'opa' on!"

But Mrs. Baxter shook her head. "Honey, if your pants split any more, *everyone's* going to see your opa."

As her parents argued, Raven spun a 180 and raced back across the restaurant floor.

Man, that was a close call! she thought as she

ducked under her table. But when she came out the other side, she had a surprise waiting.

"Opa!" cried the waiters.

Raven really had only one thing to say as she found herself swept back into the middle of the restaurant—

"Ohhhhhhhhh-pa!"

Meanwhile, back at Mr. Slick's Love Nest, Chelsea was straightening up the living room.

"Hi," said Cory as he sheepishly walked up to her.

Earlier, Chelsea had yelled at Cory and sent him to his room. That lasted all of fifteen minutes. Now Cory was back, obviously trying to get on Chelsea's good side again.

"Cory, I told Raven I'd watch you," said Chelsea. "And I can do that whether you're alive or dead. Dead is less work."

"I know," said Cory, his head hanging low. "Eddie's mad at me, you're mad at me. I'm sorry, okay?"

"I'm listening," said Chelsea.

"After Eddie gets out of the shower, how about I make some popcorn and the three of us can watch a movie—" said Cory, quickly adding, "and Eddie can sit in the middle."

Chelsea studied Cory, trying to figure out if he really had changed. She wasn't totally sure yet, but she was willing to give the kid a chance to prove it.

"Okay," she told him.

With a sigh of defeat, Cory slowly shuffled into the kitchen. But as soon as he closed the door, he jumped into the air and pumped his fist in victory.

"Yeah!" he cried softly. Level One of "Trump the Fool and Kiss the Jewel" had been accomplished. Now for Level Two, he thought as he raced up the back stairs.

When he reached the bathroom, he carefully put his ear to the door. Inside, Eddie was singing in the shower. Cory knew he'd never even hear the door open and close.

Carefully, Cory crept into the room. . . .

"Yeah, smell good," Eddie rapped as he stepped out of the shower in Raven's bathroom and toweled off. "Smell good. Yeah, all right."

Suddenly, he stopped and looked again at the corner of the floor where he'd left his clothes. Something didn't look right about that pile.

When he took a closer look, he nearly hit the ceiling. His clothes were gone! Cory had obviously replaced them with his own. And these weren't even Cory's *clothes*, they were his little white flannel dinosaur *pajamas*!

"Cory!"

Eddie lunged for the door, but it was stuck. He tried pulling it again and again. But he couldn't get it open more than an inch. Through the crack, he saw something tied to the doorknob on the other side.

Banging on the door, he yelled, "If you don't open this door you little rat . . . !"

On the other side, Cory snickered as he tied the other end of Raven's pantyhose to her bed.

Level Two of Cory's mission was now complete. Chelsea, baby, he sang to himself as he danced down the steps, your Mr. Wonderful is on his way!

Trapped in Raven's bathroom, Eddie finally stopped pulling, banging, and yelling.

With a sigh, he walked over to the pile of Cory's pajamas. He picked up the teeny little pants and teeny little top. The fluffy white flannel was covered with colorful triceratops and T. rex.

Eddie sighed in disgust, but he knew he had no choice. Holding his breath, he squeezed into both. The pajama bottoms looked more like bike pants, stretching barely to his knees. And the top was so small it looked like he was wearing a midriff shirt.

Catching sight of himself in the full-length mirror, Eddie shook his head.

"Man," he said. "I'm gonna kill him."

But first Eddie had to escape the bathroom. All he had to do was make a rope out of some towels and climb out the window. So how hard could that be?

Meanwhile, back at the restaurant, the Greek dancing was in full swing.

"Opa!" cried Matthew as he sprang to his feet and threw his hands in the air.

Across the room, Mr. Baxter jumped to *his* feet. "Opa!" he yelled.

Opa—no! Raven thought in horror as her dad joined the circle of dancers. He's going to see me now for sure, she realized.

Trapped in the circle, Raven had to think fast. With one sharp tug, she pulled a table-cloth cleanly off a nearby table for two. But before she could wrap the blue linen around herself to hide, she felt the entire room freeze—

Through her eye
The vision runs
Flash of future
Here it comes—

I see Chelsea in our living room. The phone is ringing. She's answering it— "Hello?" she says into the receiver.

Uh-oh. Whoever's on the other end of that line is making Chelsea really nervous. Now she's saying something else— "Oh, hi, Mrs. Baxter . . ."

Coming out of her vision, Raven immediately panicked. According to her vision, her mother was about to call home and check up on her.

Raven had to warn Chelsea not to answer the phone. All the girl had to do was let the answering machine pick up, then her mother would just think they were busy with their beauty treatments or watching a movie, anything but the truth—that Raven wasn't there!

Wrapping the blue tablecloth around her body and the bottom of her face, Raven looked like an Arabian princess dancing toward the restroom area. But when she tried to move out of the dancer's circle, her annoying date jumped right in front of her!

"Opa!" cried Matthew, plowing into her and sending her into the middle of the dance circle.

Knowing her father was right behind her, Raven held tightly to the tablecloth and tried to kick her feet as if she were dancing.

Very shrewdly, she inched backward until she was dancing right in front of her father. Then with one quick move, she threw the tablecloth backward, right over his head—and made a dash for the other side of the room.

"Opa!" cried Matthew, blocking her exit again.

But Raven was out of patience. "O-*please!*" she snapped at Matthew, tossing her head. Then she pushed the boy aside and headed out of the dining room.

Matthew just shrugged and moved to the middle of the circle. Mr. Baxter was already there, pulling the tablecloth off his head.

"Opa!" they cried to each other like long lost buddies.

Then, Raven's father kicked up his heels and began to dance with Raven's date.

Chapter Five

With Eddie still trapped in Raven's bathroom, Cory was ready for the next phase of his plan.

He waited patiently in the living room for Chelsea to come out of the kitchen. When she did, Cory sprang into action, pulling the front door wide open.

"C'mon, Eddie, don't be mad!" he pretended to call down the street. "Eddie!"

"Eddie left?" asked Chelsea. She stood in the middle of the living room, a bowl of popcorn in her hands and a look of distress on her face.

"Yeah, he's still mad," said Cory with a theatrical sigh. "I'm sorry, I'm such a jerk," he added, shutting the door and dragging himself across the room dejectedly.

Chelsea felt bad. "No, Cory, you're just a kid," she told him, patting the top of his head. "C'mon," she said, taking his hand in hers to cheer him up, "let's go watch that movie."

Cory looked at Chelsea with his patented big-puppy-dog eyes. Then he hit her with his hurt-little-boy voice. "You won't be ashamed to sit on the same couch with me?"

"No," Chelsea replied, falling for Cory's act.

Just as they were turning to head for the couch, Cory saw Eddie. He was dangling outside the living room window, hanging by the knots on his towel rope.

Uh-oh, thought Cory. Tightening his grip on Chelsea's hand, he spun her all the way around until she faced the kitchen.

"I'll start the movie," he announced, pushing her toward the kitchen doors. "You get the sodas."

"Cory!" cried Chelsea, annoyed. She was sure he was up to something again—she just didn't know what.

"Get the sodas, be happy!" he cried.

Shaking her head, she headed out of the living room. And Cory immediately ran to the window.

"I'm gonna get you!" cried Eddie, reaching to push open the window from his towel rope.

But Cory wasn't going to let that happen anytime soon. With one little flick, he'd locked the window tight—and Eddie lost his balance, falling to the ground.

In a flash, Eddie was up again and dashing for the front door. With one lunge, Cory locked the door tight, too. A split-second later, Eddie reached the knob and howled in frustration.

"Who's the man now, baby?" taunted Cory.

With his face pressed against the door's frosted glass, Eddie watched the little brat do a victory dance.

Keep dancing, you little pit bull, thought Eddie. 'Cause I'm going to get you—even if it takes all night!

Meanwhile, in the kitchen, Chelsea reached to pick up the ringing phone.

"Hello? Oh, hi, Raven. How's the date going?"

On the other end of the line, Raven was in a panic. "Girl, don't talk," she said breathlessly, "just listen. I had a vision. Whatever you do, do not pick up the phone."

Beep-beep went the receiver in Chelsea's ear.

"Ah, wait, wait, wait, hold on," she told Raven, "there's call-waiting."

Raven freaked when she heard Chelsea

picking up the incoming call. "Chelsea! No!" she cried. But it was too late.

"Hello?" said Chelsea, "Oh, hi, Mrs. Baxter. Hang on."

Chelsea clicked back to Raven's call.

"Rae, it's your mom. She wants to know where you are."

Raven held her breath. Okay, she thought, this is not a disaster—*yet*. "Um . . . tell her I'm on my way to the bathroom."

"Oh, good one," said Chelsea. She grinned in relief as she clicked the line back to Raven's mother. "Uh, Mrs. Baxter? Raven's on her way to the bathroom. . . ."

After Mrs. Baxter responded, Chelsea said, "Okay," then she clicked back to Raven's call. "Rae, she told me to tell you that you look really nice tonight." Chelsea was still grinning, but a second later her face fell. "How would she know *that*?"

Suddenly, Raven felt a prickly sensation on the back of her neck. Slowly, she turned around. Standing there, with her own cell phone plastered to her ear, was Raven's mother. And she did *not* look happy.

"Trust me, girl," Raven informed Chelsea, "she ain't psychic."

Wincing under her mother's intense glare, Raven said good-bye to Chelsea and turned to face Judge Judy.

"Hey, Mom," she said with a tense smile.

Her mother just stood there, her furious expression saying, "You are *so* going to pay for this."

"That was kind of funny, you know," Raven began to babble nervously. "I was on the phone, and you were on the phone, right? And, you know, not really that funny right at *this* moment. But when we look *back* on it in a couple of years, we'll be like, *that* was *funny*—"

Her mother hadn't chilled in the least. And Raven's "we'll laugh about this later" strategy wasn't helping—*at all.*

"Okay," Raven finally said, biting her lip with dread. "I'm going to shut up and let you talk."

"What is going on?" snapped her mother.

"I'm on a date," Raven admitted with a pained grimace.

"With whom?" asked her mother.

"A guy named Matthew. . . . You don't exactly know him."

"Well, that's one point against you," said Mrs. Baxter. "Keep going."

"Actually, I really didn't know him all that well, either. I mean, if I knew he was so disgusting, I would have never gone out with him in the first place. I mean, this was the worst date of my life. I thought *older* guys were supposed to be *cool.*"

"So," snapped her mother, "you went out with an *older* boy you *don't know*? Two points. Keep going."

Her mother's little mental scorecard was freaking Raven out, but she had no choice. She continued, "Well, after you guys left, he picked me up to go out to dinner."

Her mother looked like Mount Vesuvius about two seconds before an eruption. "And you *rode* with him in a *car*?"

"Yeah, I know," said Raven with a sigh. "Three points."

"No, actually that's *ten points*," said Mrs. Baxter, her tone switching to what sounded like a *really* ticked off game-show host. "And now here's Mom to tell you what you've won."

"Oh, a ride home?" asked Raven hopefully. She was more than willing to take the parental stomping if it meant getting her the heck out of Athens.

"Oh, you're going home!" cried Mrs. Baxter. "But first I want to know *why* you went out in the first place. After we said *no*?"

"Because, Mama, you wouldn't listen to me," Raven said quickly. "I was trying to explain. I mean, you never listen to *anything* I say."

"That's not true," Mrs. Baxter replied.

"Mama, yes it is. I mean, if it's not exactly what you want to hear, then you just tune me out."

"What?" said Mrs. Baxter. "I am *not* listening to this."

Raven couldn't believe her mother. She was doing it *again*!

"Mama, like that!" cried Raven, getting angry herself now.

Just then, Matthew appeared, looking for his date.

"Hey, Raven, look at me," he said. "I'm Mr. Spock."

Raven's eyes bugged out. The boy had shaped pieces of pita bread into pointy ears and slapped them on the side of his head.

Dang, Raven thought in horror, my date is acting like the biggest dork in the free world.

She spun around and faced her mother. "Mom, if you love me, you'll start dragging my sorry butt home now."

Mrs. Baxter looked first at her pleading daughter, then at her pleading daughter's pitiful date.

"I want to talk to your father first," said Mrs. Baxter, turning on her spiky red heel and heading into the dining room. "And then we'll see just how sorry your butt is."

Meanwhile, at the Baxter house, Cory had yet to put an end to Eddie's babysitting nightmare.

After locking the front door, Cory raced

to the kitchen and locked the back door, too.

With Chelsea settling into the couch in the living room, the nine-year-old now had a clear stage for his grand finale.

He opened the refrigerator. Let's see now, he thought, what can I use here?

After assembling his weapons of choice, Cory climbed onto the counter next to the open window above the sink and waited.

This was the final way into the Baxter house, and sure enough, Eddie thought he was being clever as he pushed aside the drawn blinds and began to climb through it.

"Oh, look," taunted Cory, looming over Eddie's head, "it's my date for the evening."

Looking up, Eddie froze.

"Now, remember man," warned Eddie in an alarmed voice. "I'm wearing *your* pajamas."

Cory didn't care. He just let loose—first the eggs and then the oatmeal. By the time he was through, Eddie's head looked like it was ready for the oven. And Cory's pajamas were definitely ready for the trash.

But Cory didn't care. He never liked those kiddie pajamas anyway!

Chapter Six

"**W**here are you going?" Matthew asked Raven as she strode back into the restaurant's dining room and grabbed her coat off the back of her chair.

"Home. With my parents," Raven informed him, "'Cause, oops, I forgot to tell you . . . I'm *fourteen*."

Matthew looked genuinely surprised.

"I know, it's hard to believe," said Raven, striking a pose—'cause she knew she *definitely* looked good tonight. But the night was *definitely* over!

"Buh-bye," she told him. Then she crossed the dining room to her parents' table.

"I'm glad you're getting the check," she told

her parents, "'cause I am *so* ready to go."

Mr. Baxter gave Raven a funny look.

"Uh, actually," he said, "your mother and I talked and decided . . ."

Raven waited. *What?* she wanted to scream. What have you decided about my life *now*?

"*He's* your ride home," finished Mr. Baxter, pointing across the room to Matthew.

Raven's jaw dropped. She glanced back at her date. He was holding his soda glass *and* his water glass to his lips, trying to see if he could drink from both at once.

He looked like a total moron.

"You wanted this date, you got this date," her mother told her.

Raven could not believe this was happening. She wanted to cry. "Man," she squeaked, "are you all serious? He is *disgusting*."

"Yeah, well, maybe you'll think twice before you lie to us again," said Mr. Baxter.

"Oh," said Raven. She understood perfectly—this was her punishment. But, dang! This was cruel and unusual!

Her head hanging in defeat, Raven slunk back across the dining room.

"Hey, you know what?" Matthew told her when she returned to their table. "I've been thinking. So what if you're fourteen. Your parents just ordered us the Super Duper Opa!"

Raven was almost scared to ask. But she did. "Super Duper Opa?"

Just then, the gigantic ice-cream sundae arrived at their table, along with a group of waiters who shouted a great big "Opa!" and then plunked the ton of ice cream, syrup, and whipped cream down right in front of Matthew.

"Opa!" called Raven's parents, raising their glasses at their table.

"I don't want to be a pig," said Matthew, handing her a utensil the size of a garden shovel. "So you can get the spoon."

Then he dug into the giant mound of vanilla ice cream and chocolate syrup with his *fingers*!

"Don't just look at it. Eat it!" he cried, shoving gobs of ice cream into his mouth.

And now for another episode of Doubtful Dining Decorum, thought Raven with a shudder. She glanced over at her parents—her father was laughing and her mother looked horrified.

Look away, Mama, thought Raven. Just look away.

Thirty minutes later, the Super Duper Opa was finished. Matthew's cheeks, chin, and shirt were covered in melted ice cream. And Mr. Baxter seemed completely satisfied that Raven was completely miserable.

Mrs. Baxter might have been just as satisfied, but about halfway through the ice-cream carnage, she *had* finally looked away.

Mr. Baxter leaned toward his wife. "Okay, you can look now," he told her. "He's finished."

"Did you see the way he *attacked* that thing? It was like feeding time at the zoo!" cried Mrs. Baxter.

At last, Raven dragged herself over to her parents table, her pride completely crushed.

"If you love me, you'll take me home now," she said flatly.

"Okay, fine," said Mr. Baxter. "But first, we're going to go over a few rules. Now, look, I understand you're getting older and you want your independence, but lying to us is not the way."

"Got it," said Raven.

"But," added Mrs. Baxter in a softer voice,

"your father and I also realize that not taking the time to listen to you is also not cool."

Raven looked up, a ray of hope shining in her big brown eyes. "So, you're saying that this date is, like, officially *over*? I don't have to ride home with him, do I?"

Mrs. Baxter smiled. "Sweetheart, you were *never* going to ride home with him."

"Really?" said Raven. She nodded, impressed. "You guys are good."

"And we just keep getting better," said Mr. Baxter.

Raven and her parents crossed the room to speak to Matthew. He looked totally bloated—and a little sick—from the big meal and giant sundae.

"It was very nice meeting you," said Mr. Baxter. "Don't bother about getting up . . . not that you could."

As they turned to leave, Raven shook her

head in amazement. "Where does he put it all?" she wondered.

"I don't know," said Raven's dad, glancing over his shoulder. "But we better get out of here before he decides to put it all *back*."

When Raven and her parents finally arrived home, they found Cory asleep on the couch.

On the drive back, Raven had talked to Chelsea and Eddie on her cell and heard all about Cory's Mr. Slick antics.

Raven told her parents how Cory had acted, and Mr. and Mrs. Baxter vowed to have a stern talk with their son when they got home. But when they saw Cory asleep on the couch, they changed their minds.

"I don't know," Chelsea told them all with a shrug, "he just passed out ten minutes into the movie."

Mrs. Baxter nodded. Gazing down at her

slumbering "angel baby," it was hard for her to remember he'd been acting like a little devil. Mrs. Baxter was also tired. She was ready for bed herself.

"Let's let him sleep," she whispered. Then she kissed Cory's forehead and headed for the stairs. "Good night."

"Chelsea, c'mon," said Mr. Baxter, "I'll drive you home."

Raven hugged her friend. "I'll tell you about it tomorrow," she said.

Chelsea nodded and walked toward the front door with Mr. Baxter.

"That's a really lovely look for you, Mr. Baxter," said Chelsea, raising an eyebrow at the red shawl still wrapped around the seat of his pants.

Mr. Baxter was actually too tired to think of a comeback. He just shot Raven a "your friend's pushing her luck" look before he shut the door.

After they'd gone, Raven stared down at her baby brother. He did look like a little angel—but she still thought he deserved a lesson.

Nudging his small shoulder, Raven called, "Hey, Cory, wake up. Someone wants to give you a good-night kiss."

"Chelsea?" murmured Cory dreamily.

Nope, not *that* babysitter, Raven thought with a smile. The *other* one!

Suddenly, Eddie burst through the kitchen doors, two full cans of whipped cream in his hands.

"Pucker up, precious!" he cried. Then Cory got a faceful of whipped cream.

Raven laughed. Oh, yeah, she thought, now *that's* what I call a just dessert!

Part Two

Chapter One

It was a sunny Monday morning at Bayside Junior High and Raven Baxter was trying to keep a sunny attitude. Unfortunately, she was sitting in the "Terminator's" classroom, where "sunny" was rarely in the forecast.

"All right, class," said Mr. Petracelli, "here's one that everyone should know, but few do. The first capital of our country was . . . ?"

I know this one! Raven thought. She raised her hand along with two other students.

The history teacher sighed as he looked over his classroom. While three students obviously knew the answer, most remained hunched over their desks in an empty-headed daze.

"Ah, the chosen few," he muttered, eyeing the students who'd raised their hands.

Raven raised hers even higher. Call on me, call on me! she tried to psychically communicate. C'mon, Mr. P., I know the answer!

But Mr. Petracelli didn't call on Raven. He was more interested in starting his first "search and destroy" mission of the morning.

Switching to "Terminator" mode, the teacher slowly walked the aisles, scanning the students as if they were hard targets.

His gaze narrowed on a nerdy-looking boy with glasses named Larry whose hand was raised.

KISS-UP! KISS-UP! flashed in the teacher's eyes as if he were analyzing a digital readout on the kid.

Next the Terminator stared at Raven, whose hand waving was so energetic it looked like Old Glory on the Fourth of July.

SHOW OFF! flashed the teacher's read-out.

Finally he came to Kenny Brookwell. "Head Cold Kenny" was one of those unfortunate members of the student body whose hand almost never saw any altitude.

Mr. Petracelli eyed the Game Boy in Kenny's hands and concluded: CLUELESS, UNPREPARED, DESTROY!

"Mister Brookwell," said Mr. Petracelli, calling on Kenny.

The boy panicked—then sneezed. His nickname was Head Cold Kenny for a very good reason. The kid was constantly sick!

"I'm dorry. I dote know," Kenny answered through his stuffy nose.

"I'm dorry you dote know, too," said the teacher.

Raven watched the whole scene in frustration. She popped her head into Mr. Petracelli's line of sight. "But I do, all right?" she reminded him, her hand still waving.

The teacher looked right past Raven and instead zeroed in on her best friend Eddie Thomas.

Eddie didn't have his hand raised. And he had *gum* in his mouth—one of Mr. P.'s many classroom no-no's.

"No gum chewing" came right after "no cell phones or beepers," and right before "no talking back."

The Terminator glared at Eddie.

With a nervous gulp, Eddie swallowed the evidence.

"Mr. Thomas," barked the teacher. "Seems like you've had time to *chew* on this one."

"Uh . . ." said Eddie.

"No," Mr. Petracelli told Eddie. "*Uh* is the capital of *Duh*, which you seem to be the *mayor* of."

Raven was still waving her hand in the air. "Hey, just in case you didn't know," she announced to the teacher, "my hand is up over here. All right? Just letting you know!"

Mr. Petracelli totally ignored her. He continued to loom over Eddie.

Beads of sweat formed on Eddie's upper lip as he said, "Why don't we let Raven take this one?"

"I didn't ask her, I asked you," said Mr. Petracelli.

Then he returned to the front of the classroom and said, "The answer, class, is Philadelphia." He punctuated this announcement with a roll of his neck, which sent a cracking sound through the whole classroom.

Raven leaned across the aisle and whispered to Eddie, "I hate how he only calls on people who don't have their hands raised."

"And that cracking sound is *nasty*," Eddie

added. "My grandmother does that with her toes."

At the front of the room, Mr. Petracelli posed his next question. "Now, many people attribute *this* scientific advance to Benjamin Franklin, but it was really made by Michael Faraday."

The Terminator scanned the class once more. A few students had raised their hands. But they were the usual suspects, so he wasn't interested in them.

Then he noticed Raven. This time, she didn't have her hand raised. Instead, she was frantically skimming the pages of the open textbook on her desk.

Immediately, the history teacher's Terminator scanning mode kicked in: FAST HEARTBEAT, INCREASED RESPIRA-TION . . .

Finally came the verdict: DEAD DUCK.

"I just had a vision of my parents saying, 'no!'" Raven told Chelsea.

"Where was I again?" Mr. Baxter said to Raven.
"Oh, yeah. *No!*"

"But she'll be able to make it *Saturday* night,"
Raven said, pretending to be Chelsea.

"Our first night together, baby," Cory said.

"They're going out," Raven said, pulling off her shower cap, "and so am I."

Eww, gross! Raven thought.

"Whatever you do, do not pick up
the phone," Raven told Chelsea.

"So, you're saying that this date is, like,
officially *over*?" Raven said hopefully.

Part Two

"What's so great about being near *that* water fountain?" Raven asked Eddie.

"I need a master in deceit...."
Raven said to her brother.

"I'm sorry, Daddy,"
Cory said sweetly.

"I'm gonna need that five
bucks back," Raven said.

"Oh, you got me a phone!" cried Raven.

"My daughter is in a bit of a jam. . . ."
Raven (in her Mama Baxter disguise) told Eddie.

"We were just saying how *responsible* Raven's become," Mrs. Baxter said.

"I just have one question," said Mrs. Baxter. "When you put this on, exactly *what* mother were you thinking of?"

"Miss Baxter?" said the teacher, calling on her.

Raven swallowed. "I don't have my hand up," she said nervously.

"Exactly," said the teacher.

Raven frowned. "Mr. Petracelli, when my hand is up, I *know* the answer. And when my hand is down, I *don't* know the answer. Let me explain again, hand up—*know*. Hand down—*don't*."

In the dead silence that followed, Raven realized that she might have come dangerously close to breaking the man's "no talking back" rule. So she quickly gave an innocent shrug and added, "I'm just saying."

"No," the teacher responded, "you're 'just saying' everything but the answer, which is *electricity*. Which led to the light bulb. Which is obviously not going off in your head."

But in the next moment, something *else* went off in Raven's head—a vision.

Through her eye
The vision runs
Flash of future
Here it comes—

I see myself in the school hallway.

Whoa! There are all these kids from my history class standing around me clapping and cheering.

Ohmigosh! They're cheering for ME!

Now I'm spinning around, hearing each of them compliment me.

Larry is saying, "All right, Raven!"

Now Brendan is saying, "You really told Petracelli off!"

Eddie is smiling and clapping, and so is Head Cold Kenny. . . .

When Raven came out of her vision, she could see Mr. Petracelli was still talking to her.

". . . So, unless you have anything else to waste class time with—"

"As a matter of fact, I do," said Raven, rising to her feet. The vision she'd just had of the entire history class cheering for her had given her the confidence she needed to really give this teacher what he had coming.

Holding her head high, she looked the Terminator in the eye and said, "Why do you only call on people who don't have their hand raised?"

Mr. Petracelli did *not* look happy. "Whom I call on is my choice," he said sternly. "Sit down."

Raven didn't.

"But see. I had my hand up plenty of times today, and you only called on me when I didn't know the answer. And I know why," she said, waving her hand in the air to make her point. "Because you have more fun *embarrassing* us than *teaching* us. And trust me, the whole class has my back on this right here."

Raven expected the entire class to stand up and cheer. But they didn't. Instead, every single student slid his or her desk *away* from Raven—in unison.

Uh-oh, thought Raven. Was my vision totally bogus?

"Oh, well," she said, just a *teensy* bit less confident. "This is probably the wrong time to be talking about this, right? Right. And maybe, you know, after school, we could just toss it around a little bit. You know, toss it around."

"Good idea," said the teacher with a grimace. "Why don't you and I 'toss it around' tomorrow after school? And hey, let's 'toss in' your *parents*, too?"

When the bell rang, Raven trudged into the hallway outside, totally defeated.

Suddenly, she was surrounded by all the kids from her history class. They were clapping and cheering—just like her vision.

"All right, Raven!" cried Larry.

"You really told Petracelli off!" said Brendan.

Eddie was smiling and clapping, too. And so was Head Cold Kenny.

Traitors, she wanted to scream. You're all a bunch of spineless chickens. Where were you when I needed you?

Finally, Raven noticed Kenny giving her a thumbs up and stepping toward her to offer his thanks. But instead of words, he accidentally let out a big, wet, sloppy sneeze—all over her!

Oh, great, thought Raven, a perfectly awful end to a perfectly awful class. And with the Terminator totally steamed at her, Raven knew future forecasts for *this* classroom weren't about to get any sunnier.

Chapter Two

"**H**ey, my parents have to meet with Petracelli, and they are going to freak," Raven told Eddie as she walked with him to his locker. "How am I going to tell them?"

"Just fake being sick," said Eddie. He opened his locker to exchange a few books. "They can't get mad if you're sick."

"I stopped doing that kind of stuff when I was eight," Raven told him. Then she thought for a minute . . . "It's brilliant," she said.

"Yeah, and I've got a great recipe for fake vomit," said Eddie. "A little bit of creamed corn, some yogurt, and some dog food. And if you pop it in the oven at 350 degrees, it'll actually steam."

Raven shuddered. She didn't know if she wanted to go *that* far.

Just then, a big, tall kid brushed past Eddie. "'Scuse me," said the giant as he threw a book hard into Eddie's locker. He was holding a sandwich in his mouth and a half-eaten bag of chips in his hand. He put both inside the locker, too.

Eddie was outraged. "Say, brother! That's *my* locker!"

But the giant obviously didn't care. "I know," he said. "I had it last year. It's a good location. Right next to the water fountain." The big kid pointed to the water fountain on the wall a few feet away.

"But there are lots of water fountains," said Eddie, totally confused.

"I like this one," said the big guy. And not very nicely. Then he slammed the locker and strode away.

Eddie was floored. "You can't do this!" he called. "I know my rights!"

But the giant just kept walking.

"I don't get it," said Raven. "What's so great about being near *that* water fountain?"

Just then, a pretty girl left the classroom right next door and stepped up to the fountain to take a drink.

"Exhibit A," said Eddie.

After school, Raven still wasn't sure what to do about Mr. Petracelli's demand for a parent–teacher meeting. So she took her problem to the one person she knew could help.

"Fake vomit is great, but I need more," Raven explained. "I need a master in deceit and the art of psychological manipulations. That's why I came to you."

"You made a wise choice," said nine-year-old Cory Baxter, swiveling in his desk chair to face his older sister. "I'm going to need that five bucks up front."

Raven rose from Cory's bunk bed and slapped a bill into the boy's palm. Instantly, he held it up to the light to make sure it was on the up and up.

"It's cool," said Cory. He pocketed the payment, and Raven sat back down on his bunk bed. With her fuzzy pen poised over her notebook, she waited for Cory's first lesson in the art of parental deception.

"Now," Cory began, "this little trick works on Mom and Dad every time."

Using his back scratcher as a pointer, he revealed a little sign he'd made. "I call it 'The Three Cs,'" he explained.

"What does that stand for?" asked Raven. "Crazy, Creepy, and Constipated?"

"That was *one* night!" cried Cory, annoyed. "Now do you want my help or not?"

"Okay, I'm sorry. The Three Cs are . . . ?"

"Cuddle. Compliment. And the ever-popular Cry," said Cory, pointing to the words on his homemade sign.

"Wait a second," said Raven. "That's what got you out of burning the Christmas tree in '98?"

"Yep. I *cuddled* up in Mom's arms, *complimented* Dad on the great job he did on the Christmas lights, and I even worked up a little tear." Cory pointed to his cheek. "Right here."

Raven quickly scribbled Cory's advice into her notebook. She was impressed. Her little brother had taken his skills to a new high—*er*, make that *low*.

"And they still gave you that new bike," she recalled.

"And a basketball," said Cory. "Yeah, '98 was a good year."

"Cory Baxter!" Mrs. Baxter called from

downstairs. She did *not* sound happy. "Get down here right now!"

Cory shuddered and turned to Raven. "Okay, I really screwed up in school today. You might want to take notes."

"Do you know who I just got off the phone with?" Mrs. Baxter snapped at her son. "Your teacher. You have been acting up in class again."

Cory was sitting at the kitchen table getting a lecture from his mother. Raven sat nearby, her pen poised once again to take notes on how to avoid parental punishment.

Their dad was standing by the stove, cooking dinner.

"Victor," called Mrs. Baxter over her shoulder, "talk to your son."

Mr. Baxter left the stove and walked over to the table where Cory was sitting. "Cory—" he began calmly, until Mrs. Baxter pulled him aside.

"*Angry* voice," she murmured.

"Cory!" Mr. Baxter repeated, but in a deeper voice this time. "We are very disappointed in you."

Cory looked up with big, blinking eyes. "I'm sorry, Daddy," he said sweetly. Then Cory rose and hugged his father.

"Aww—" said his father, melting.

But Mrs. Baxter wasn't falling for Cory's fake out. And she was ticked off that her husband *had*. She pinched her husband's arm.

"—Ow!" cried Mr. Baxter.

"Stay with me," she told her husband. Then she turned to Cory and said, "Don't you go *cuddling* up to him or giving us any of your lame *compliments*. And don't you even think about *crying*. Or you're going to see a side of me that's not very pretty."

"Mother, how is that possible when you're

so beautiful," gushed Cory with a teddy-bear innocent smile.

"Oh, knock it off and go to your room," snapped Mrs. Baxter. Then she returned to the counter to help Mr. Baxter finish preparing dinner.

Dang, thought Raven, shaking her head. Her mom sure got the 4-1-1 on Cory's Three Cs.

As her brother walked by on his way out, Raven ripped the "Cory's Advice on Parental Deception" page out of her notebook and tossed it to him.

"I'm gonna need that five bucks back," she said.

With a sheepish shrug, Cory dug into his pocket and refunded her money. Then he headed up the back stairs to his room.

"What's gotten into him lately?" said her mother. "He's always acting up with his teachers."

"Don't be too hard on him, Mom," said Raven. "He's just a kid, and kids make mistakes."

And please, please, please remember that when I have to tell you about my own mistake in Mr. Petracelli's class, thought Raven.

Mrs. Baxter gave Raven a funny look. Then she turned to her husband and said, "Was she just defending her brother?"

"I think so," he said. "I gotta sit down. The room is spinning."

"You know what I think we're seeing here? A more mature, responsible young lady. The new Raven," said Mrs. Baxter, with pride in her voice.

Raven felt like crawling into a hole. "Well, it's not the new Raven," she tried to tell them. "It's the same old Raven."

"Your grades have been good," her mother pointed out, "you've been helping out around the house—"

"And I can't remember the last time we were called down to the school because you were, I don't know, mouthing off about something," added her father.

"Don't you miss it?" asked Raven nervously. "I mean, all those really good times? I messed up and you got mad. Wheeee!"

Her parents just laughed.

"Anyhow," said Mrs. Baxter, "we're so proud of you that we have a little something for you."

"Really?" Raven remembered the furious look on Mr. Petracelli's face and swallowed uneasily. "I hope it's a *very* little something."

Her father grinned. "We were going to wait for your birthday, but now is a great time."

Raven sighed. With a furrowed brow she followed her parents out of the kitchen and up the back stairs, thinking the whole way, *If you only knew . . .*

* * *

Minutes later, Raven was being led into her attic bedroom by her father. Her mother had her hands over Raven's eyes.

"And now, the greatest present a teenage girl could ever want," announced her father.

"Ooh, you got me a Los Angeles Laker?" said Raven, feeling the air in front of her. "'Cause you know I like 'em tall."

"Here you go, baby," said her mother, finally removing her hands from Raven's eyes.

There, nestled in her father's big palms, was a lavender cordless phone.

"Oh, you got me a phone!" cried Raven.

"With your own phone number," her father told her.

"And I even programmed the speed dial for you," said her mother. "Your best friend in the whole world is number one. Go ahead, try it!"

"Okay," said Raven. She pushed the button, expecting to hear Chelsea Daniels or Eddie

Thomas picking up on the other end of the line. Instead, her *mother's* cell phone rang.

"Hey, girlfriend!" cried Mrs. Baxter into the phone—a little *too* excitedly.

C'mon, Mom, chill, okay? thought Raven.

Mr. Baxter leaned close. "I'll show you how to delete it later," he whispered.

Raven sighed. She couldn't take it. This was just too much guilt for one girl to handle. She had to come clean. "Ah . . . Mom. Dad. You know, I don't really know how to say this—"

"And you don't have to," said her father, cutting her off. "Just keep up the good work."

"Call me," her mother said with a laugh as she held up a pinkie and thumb to her ear.

Before Raven could psych herself up to come clean, both parents had left her bedroom.

Still racked with guilt, she gazed at her parents' present. "Yay," she said with a heavy sigh.

Later that night, Raven used her new phone to call Eddie.

"Rae, just hang up and go tell them the truth," Eddie advised her. "They'll understand."

"Not after they told me how proud they were of me. No way!" she cried. "Okay, to them, I'm the 'new Raven.' And the 'new Raven' doesn't mess up."

"So what's the *new* Raven going to do?" asked Eddie.

"Well, I'm just going to have to go to Mr. Petracelli. Talk to him, no parents, one-on-one," she said.

Suddenly, Raven froze, and time seemed to stand still—

Through her eye
The vision runs
Flash of future
Here it comes—

I see myself outside my history classroom again. But this time, there are no cheering kids. Instead, I'm talking to Mr. Petracelli.

No, no, no . . . I'm wrong about that.

It's Mr. P. who's doing the talking . . . nope, wrong again. The Terminator's not talking, he's screaming.

"Go get your mother!" he's roaring. "TODAY!"

Now I'm the one whose screaming—in fear. "Ahhhhhhh!"

"Okay," Raven told Eddie as soon as she came out of her vision, "that didn't go too well. . . ."

Raven was so frustrated, she felt tears coming on. "I want my Mommy," she squeaked.

Then her gaze fell on the corner of the room. It was filled with outfits she'd designed and sewed herself, everything from her own

clothing and accessories to Halloween cos-
tumes for her family and friends.

"Mommy," Raven whispered to herself,
eyeing her seamstress's stand-up model. Maybe
she wouldn't have to see Mr. Petracelli without
a parent after all.

Chapter Three

"**L**ook at that slob," Eddie complained to a guy named Richie at school the next day. "He's disgusting."

As Eddie and Richie watched from across the hall, the giant who'd muscled in on Eddie's locker picked at the sausage and sauerkraut sandwich he'd tossed in there after lunch. Now he looked as if he was going to eat half of it and throw the rest of the stinky mess *back* into Eddie's locker so he could eat it tomorrow.

Eddie was furious. "That is my locker," he told Richie. "And if I don't take a stand now, it's going to ruin my reputation."

Just then, Mr. Petracelli passed by.

Overhearing Eddie's remark, the teacher said, "Mr. Thomas, you don't have a 'reputation.'"

Cracking his neck, the teacher kept walking.

Eddie was even angrier now. His chest puffed out, he approached the giant locker thief.

"Hey, man, we got a problem," said Eddie in his tough-guy voice.

"We do?" said the big kid.

"Yeah, I'm not sharing my locker, okay!" said Eddie sternly.

"That's cool," said the giant. He began to throw things out of the locker and onto the floor—a knapsack, a book, a hat.

Eddie was stunned. "You're throwing out *my* stuff."

"And it can go into my locker," said the big guy as he leaned down and scribbled something onto the notebook in Eddie's hand. "Here's the combination. Problem solved."

Then the big guy slammed the locker shut and walked away.

Raven was a little nervous walking out of the girls' bathroom. She'd spent half the night creating her "middle-aged mama" disguise. But now that she was wearing the fat suit, giant purple skirt, purple jacket, wig, glasses, purple hat, and fake "overbite" teeth, she wasn't sure if she could pull it off.

I've just got to act confident . . . and *old*, she told herself as she waddled along the hallway, the fat-suit disguise making her look like a 300-pound, fifty-year-old woman.

"Slow down!" she barked at a running boy in her "Mama Baxter" voice. "This is a hallway, not a freeway!"

The kid actually *did* slow down.

Dang, thought Raven. This bossy mama thing might be kind of fun.

"Eh-eh-eh, none of that!" she cried, wedging herself between a girl and boy who looked like they were about to kiss.

Then a good-looking friend of Eddie's walked by, and Raven decided to have some more fun.

First, she gave the boy a really obvious once-over. Then, in her Mama Baxter voice, she said, "Lookin' good, Richie," and winked at him.

Richie looked horrified—and Raven had to bite her tongue to keep from laughing.

Just then, she noticed Eddie.

Okay, thought Raven. Now for a real test.

"Well, you look like a fine young student," she told Eddie, whistling words through her fake overbite. "Would you please point me to Mr. Petracelli's class?"

"One floor down," said Eddie politely. "First door to your left."

"Aren't you a nice young man?" said Raven

as Mama Baxter. Then she took Eddie's cheeks in her hands and squeezed. "Look at them cheeks!"

"C'mon," complained Eddie, trying to twist away. "No pinching the cheeks!"

Laughing, Raven let go of his cheeks and pulled out her fake teeth. "It's me, Eddie. Raven!"

"Raven?" asked Eddie, stunned.

"No, I am Tanya Baxter, Raven's mother," Raven loudly announced in the hallway after putting her teeth back in. "My daughter is in a bit of a jam, and I'm here to bail her out. All right?"

As she and Eddie walked down the hall, Raven saw Richie again. "I'm comin' back for you," she teased. Then she swung her fat-suit rear, bumping him in the behind and sending him—*slam!*—into a bank of lockers.

Richie shuddered. One close encounter

with the flirtatious Mama Baxter was bad enough, but *two* was downright freaky. Rubbing his bruised leg, he couldn't limp away fast enough!

"Come on, Eddie, let's go," said Raven and they headed for Mr. Petracelli's classroom.

"You don't even look like your mom," Eddie told Raven, looking over her fat suit. "You look more like you *ate* your mom."

"Relax, Eddie, okay," said Raven. "Petracelli has never met my mother. I'll just get in, tell him Raven's grounded for life, and then I will *un*-ground myself."

When they reached the Terminator's classroom door, Raven turned to Eddie. "All right, I'm going to go in to see Mr. Petracelli. I want you to count to ten, knock on the door, and say that there's an emergency at home and I have a phone call."

Raven took a deep breath and waddled into her history classroom.

"Well, hello there, Mr. Petracelli," she said through her Mama Baxter overbite. "I'm Tanya Baxter, Raven's mother."

Mr. Petracelli rose from his desk and shook Raven's hand. "Thanks for coming," he told her.

"Anything for my baby's favorite teacher," said Raven. Then she tried to take a seat. But when she attempted to put the giant rubbery rear of her fat suit into a student desk chair, it wouldn't fit.

C'mon, she thought, get in there!

Again, she tried to shove her big bottom into the desk chair. But it *still* wouldn't fit. The third time, she did a little hop, thinking she could *lift* the bottom in.

Unfortunately, the rubber bounced instead, sending Raven down to the tiled floor.

No worries, no worries, she told herself, rolling around the floor in the fat suit. Finally, she struggled to her feet again. Adjusting her purple jacket and hat, she faced the teacher.

"So, I know this is about my baby getting talkative in class," she said. "And she assures me she's very sorry, and it'll never ever happen again."

All right, thought Raven, *that* should do it. Now where the heck is Eddie's interruption? "Is that someone knocking?" she asked hopefully.

"I didn't hear anything," said Mr. Petracelli. "Mrs. Baxter, *where's* Raven?"

"Raven . . . is . . . out in the car," said Mama Baxter. "*Crying* . . . crying her little eyes out."

Whaddya know, thought Raven. Cory's "Three Cs" lecture might be good for something after all.

"Big, puffy, red things," Mama Baxter

continued. "Runny nose. Even a face a mother wouldn't look at. . . . Well, I'm sure I heard someone—KNOCKING!"

"There is no one there," Mr. Petracelli assured her a second time. *"Now,"* he said, "I need to speak with you and Raven *together.*"

Raven could tell her teacher was losing patience. "When would you want that, Mr. Petracelli?" she asked sweetly.

"When?" he said. "Let me check my calendar. NOW!"

Raven shuddered. "Okay then, I'll see what I can do!" She waddled her Mama Baxter body out of the classroom.

Where the heck was Eddie? she wondered as she searched the halls. She found him nearby, leaning up against a locker with a dazed look on his face, watching two pretty girls talking.

Raven was furious. "Knock, knock," she said.

"Who's there?" asked Eddie innocently.

"NOT YOU!" she screamed in his ear. *Now* are you awake? she thought as she stormed off.

Chapter Four

With Mr. Petracelli still waiting to see Raven, Mama Baxter had to transform fast.

As quickly as she could, Raven waddled into the nearest girls' room.

Two students were applying makeup at the mirror. Raven frowned when she saw them. She really didn't want any witnesses to her transformation from Mama Baxter back into Raven Baxter.

So how do I get them out of here? she wondered for a moment.

"Excuse me," she finally announced as Mama Baxter, "but I think the mayonnaise on the sardine sandwich I ate for lunch was bad, so I want to apologize for any discomfort I may cause you young ladies. . . . If you have perfume, I'd spray it *now*."

In horror, the girls threw their cosmetics back into their makeup bags and rushed for the exit.

Raven rubbed her hands together with satisfaction. Nothing cleared a public bathroom faster than the threat of toxic stink!

Five minutes later, Raven was exiting the girls' room as herself. She raced up to Eddie, who was waiting outside.

Raven's fat suit, hat, glasses, and fake teeth were gone. Now she was wearing the clothes she'd had on in school that day—jeans, a sweater, and a multicolored satin jacket.

"Okay, how do I look?" she asked Eddie as she smoothed out the wrinkles in her jacket.

"You have your mother's hair," said Eddie, pointing to her head.

Raven smiled, flattered by what she thought

was a compliment. "You know, I've been told that," she gushed.

"No, no!" cried Eddie, pointing to the wig on her head. "You have your *mother's* hair."

Raven reached up and felt her head. The short, curly, gray-streaked wig was still up there all right! She yanked it off.

"Oh, okay, okay, does my hair look okay now?" she asked, smoothing down her braids.

Eddie nodded. "I'll meet you back here after I check out my new locker. Good luck."

As Eddie moved down the hallway, he counted off the locker numbers. But when he got to the locker that was now supposed to be his, he found a geeky kid putting *his* books into it.

"Is this your locker?" Eddie asked Larry.

"Not really," said Larry pushing up his glasses and shrugging his thin shoulders.

"Mine's on the third floor. Some big guy took it and made me come here."

"You, too?" Eddie couldn't believe it. This giant locker thief was out of control.

Just then, another geeky-looking kid walked up and put his books in the same locker. "Hey, Larry," he said.

"Hey, Brendan," said Larry.

"Wait a minute," said Eddie. "You mean to tell me you both share this locker?"

"Yeah," said Larry. "That guy has stolen all the good lockers."

"Mine was right next to the snack machine," said Brendan, shaking his head.

"This is crazy!" cried Eddie, now completely fed up. "We can't let him get away with this. We outnumber him, y'all. We need to take some action."

Finally, a third nerdy student approached with an armload of books.

"Hey, Leland," said Larry with a wave. Then he pointed to Eddie. "This guy wants to get our lockers back, like you tried to do."

Leland's eyes widened in fear. Then he shook his head "no" to Eddie as a warning.

Eddie gulped as he watched the kid struggle with the gesture . . . 'cause it's not easy shaking your head "no" when you're wearing a *neck brace*.

Meanwhile, over in the history classroom, Raven was ready to confront Mr. Petracelli again—this time as herself.

"So, my mom said you wanted to see me?" asked Raven innocently.

"Yes. With her. Together. Both of you," said the teacher.

"Is that really necessary?" asked Raven. "I mean, why don't you and I just sit down—"

"Go get your mother!" he roared, just like her vision. "TODAY!"

"Ahhhhhhh!" Raven cried as she fled from the Terminator's temper and raced back to the girls' room to change again.

Ten minutes later, Mama Baxter was back in front of Mr. Petracelli's classroom, gasping for breath.

Raven had run so quickly through the hallways that she'd collided with the same custodian *twice*. The first time as Raven and the second as her mama!

"Is Raven here?" Raven finally asked the teacher through her Mama Baxter overbite. "What a shame. Why don't the two of us just talk this out?"

"No!" cried Mr. Petracelli.

"Ooh, cranky," Raven told him. "Someone needs a little nappy-nap." Then Mama Baxter left the front door of the classroom and walked down the hall.

Quickly, Raven pulled off the hat, wig, and glasses and spit out her fake teeth. Careful to hide the fat suit behind a row of file cabinets, Raven stuck her normal head into the back entrance to Mr. Petracelli's classroom and asked, "Is my mother here?"

"She just left," said the teacher.

"And why did she do that?" snapped Raven, acting annoyed. "She knows we need to talk."

"Tell her that! No. Wait. *I'll* tell her," said Mr. Petracelli, heading for the front door of his classroom.

"No, wait, I'll tell her!" shrieked Raven.

By the time the teacher reached the door of his classroom, Raven had thrown the wig, hat, and glasses back on and stuck her fake teeth back in.

"Mrs. Baxter!" called the teacher down the hall.

"You called?" said Mama Baxter, sliding up to him.

But by this time, Mr. Petracelli had had enough. "I'm a busy man, Mrs. Baxter," he told Raven. "I've talked to you, I've talked to your daughter. And now, I'm going home to talk to myself and ask why I ever became a teacher." He buried his head in his hands.

In her Mama Baxter voice Raven asked, "Well, does that mean you don't want to see me?"

"I don't have to see anyone," said the teacher, waving her away, "except maybe *my* mother."

"Good-bye, Mr. Petracelli," said Raven, then she danced out the door.

Chapter Five

Raven kept dancing all the way down the hall. She was feeling so good, she thought she could accomplish just about anything. Just then, she noticed she was passing by Eddie's locker. Eddie wasn't there—but that giant bully was.

Pushing her Mama Baxter glasses up her nose, Raven waddled right up to the kid. "I heard you stole my baby's locker," she barked.

"Look, all I—"

Raven cut the kid off with a big swing of her purse. *Whap!* She whacked him right in the shoulder.

"Whoa!" cried the bully in surprise.

"All right," said Mama Baxter, "you get your things out of there. Pronto. Am I making myself clear?"

"But—"

Whap! She whacked him again.

"Now, don't you 'but' me, boy," threatened Mama Baxter. "And if you say any of this to Eddie . . . I've got a *bigger* purse. With *buckles.* OW!"

Pleased with herself, Raven strutted her fat suit on down the hall. But she didn't get far before she felt a familiar tingle through her whole body.

**Through her eye
The vision runs
Flash of future
Here it comes—**

I see my parents.

Uh-oh . . . They're opening the door to Mr. Petracelli's classroom.

Now my father's speaking.

"We're looking for Mr. Petracelli," he's saying. "We're Raven Baxter's parents."

The moment Raven shook her head clear of her vision, she panicked. She had to get back to Petracelli's classroom—*pronto*!

Waddling over there in the fat suit would take too long, she realized. So when she noticed a kid walking his scooter in through one of the school doors, she rushed up to him.

"You're young. *Walk*," she told him as she grabbed his scooter, hopped on the back, and coasted away.

"All right! Mama's in the hall!" she cried, parting the students as she scooted by.

* * *

Meanwhile, down the hall, Eddie was about to confront the locker thief giant.

With his chest puffed out and his fists clenched, Eddie strutted up to the bully. Right behind him were Larry and Brendan.

Eddie had thought four of them would look more threatening, but Leland and his neck brace had opted out.

"All right, look," said Eddie, facing off with the bully. "The guys and I have talked this over, and although we prefer to avoid physical violence—"

"Or harsh language—" noted Brendan in a nasal tone.

"Or intimidating gestures—" added Larry, pushing up his nerdy glasses.

Eddie tensed. "I got this, guys," he told them quickly. He didn't want to lose any edge the three of them might have had.

He turned back to the bully. "Now, could

you please give us back our lockers?" he asked.

The big kid didn't look the least bit intimidated by Eddie and his crew of nerds. "You know what—" he began in a menacing tone. But what he saw next killed the words in his throat.

Behind Eddie, Mama Baxter was passing by on her scooter. Instantly, she slowed down to shoot the big bully a threatening look.

The image of a big purse with big buckles flashed across the bully's mind. A few stupid lockers just wasn't worth being wailed on by Eddie's psycho mama.

"You can have 'em," he told Eddie quickly before rushing away.

A moment later, a pretty girl stopped by the water fountain next to Eddie's locker and took a long drink.

Watching her, Eddie grinned. "Sure is good to be back home."

Raven reached the back door of her history classroom, parked the scooter, and waddled inside. She found her teacher at his desk.

"Mr. Petracelli, what are you still doing here?" she asked, dropping her hat onto one of the desks.

"Oh joy, you've returned," said the teacher. But he didn't look the least bit happy to see her. In fact, he was so disturbed, he began cracking his neck.

"Only because I was worried about you," said Raven, going to the classroom's front door and opening it wide. "Staying here all times of night, cracking your neck. What kind of life is that?"

"Mrs. Baxter, are you in the PTA?" asked the teacher worriedly.

"No," said Raven.

"Let's keep it that way!" he cried and then he disappeared out the door.

Raven was about to follow him, when she realized she'd left her hat on one of the desks. As she moved to get it, however, the back door of the classroom opened. Through it came her father and mother!

Raven panicked. She spun her giant body, waddled to the blackboard, and tried to look busy erasing it.

"'Scuse me, we're looking for Mr. Petracelli," said Raven's father, just like her vision. "We're Raven Baxter's parents."

Chapter Six

As Raven's parents moved farther into the classroom, Raven tried not to freak.

There was no way she wanted to risk facing her mom and dad dressed like Mama Baxter, so she just kept erasing the blackboard.

"Oh no, it's *Ms.* Petracelli," she informed them.

"But we got a message on our machine from a *Mister* Petracelli," said Raven's mother, confused.

"Oh, see, in the rain, I got a little cold," Raven said. Then she made a big show of coughing. "So, uh, maybe you should leave."

But Raven's parents didn't leave. Instead, her

father tried again to explain. "Um, the message on the machine said Raven was talking back."

"Talking back, speaking up," said Raven, still trying to avoid facing them. "I just call it, a big ol' misunderstanding, which brings us back to buh-bye!"

While Raven's back was turned, Mrs. Baxter waved her husband over. On the wall, she noticed a newspaper clipping with a photo of a middle-aged man. The headline beneath it read LOCAL SCHOOL'S MR. PETRACELLI HONORED FOR OUTSTANDING COMMUNITY SERVICE.

Then she pointed to "Ms. Petracelli" and mouthed "Raven" to her husband. He nodded. And they closed in.

"Still here?" muttered Raven nervously, her back still turned to them. "All right, still here, okay."

She'd completely erased the blackboard, so

she needed something else to do fast. Quickly, she crossed over to the bulletin board and pretended to read it.

"Oh, look, bake sale!" she cried.

When her mother and father followed right behind her, she veered away and walked to the other side of the room again.

"Ms. Petracelli," said Mr. Baxter, "we took off the entire afternoon to come down here."

"So we're not leaving until we get this whole thing sorted out," added Mrs. Baxter.

Raven found herself back at the blackboard. Looking for something to do, she picked up two erasers and began to clap them.

"All right," she muttered, "not gonna leave, okay, oh, okay, oh—"

As her parents drew closer, she veered again and found herself facing a tabletop globe.

"What is this doing here?" she announced. Holding it in front of her face, she crossed to the windows. "I didn't know Brazil was that big!"

"It's funny," said her mother. "We were just saying how *responsible* Raven's become."

"We even got her a new phone," added her father.

"And she loves that phone like a puppy," blurted Raven. Oops, she thought, then quickly added, "She said. To me."

Just then, the computer made a sound.

Great, thought Raven, a distraction! "Ooh look, got mail," she said, crossing the room yet again. Looking down at the computer screen, she started typing furiously.

"What bothers me the most," her mother went on, "is that if Raven was having a problem in school, why didn't she come to us about it?"

"Any thoughts about that, Ms. Petracelli?" asked her father.

Raven sighed. "Well, if I was Raven—which

I'm *not*—maybe she'd be afraid to come to you because she thinks you want her to be perfect . . . she said to me."

"We don't expect her to be perfect," said her mother.

"Yes, you do!" Raven blurted out. "You even called her the 'new Raven.'"

"Look, Ms. Petracelli, maybe we gave Raven the wrong idea," said Mrs. Baxter. "We are very proud of her, but that doesn't mean we don't expect her to mess up sometimes."

"Yeah," agreed her father, "we want her to feel like she can come to us even when she does mess up."

"And if Raven doesn't know all this," said her mother, "maybe we're not doing our jobs as parents."

Raven sighed. She felt terrible. "Raven thinks you're doing a great job," she told them.

"Really?" asked her mother.

"Really," said Raven, nodding. Reaching up, Raven pulled off her wig and turned to face her parents.

"Victor, look!" said her mother dramatically. "It's *Raven*."

"Holy cow, it is!" said her father, just as dramatically.

"Okay, okay," said Raven. Obviously, her parents had guessed she *wasn't* Ms. Petracelli. "When did you all find it out?"

Her father laughed. "When your butt went left, you went right."

"Betrayed by the booty," said Raven with a sigh as she glanced over her shoulder—and down. Her Mama Baxter assets had given her away.

That night in her bedroom, Raven was forced to have one last heart-to-heart talk.

"Look," she said, "I know I disappointed

you, but will you please stop staring at me like that?"

Mr. Baxter waited for his daughter to say good-bye to her phone. But it really seemed ridiculous to him. "We're only taking the phone away for two weeks," he reminded her.

"I know," said Raven, gazing at her beautiful new lavender phone, "but it looks so sad."

Mr. Baxter just shook his head, picked up the phone, and left.

"Call me . . . !" Raven cried to her departing phone.

As her father went out the bedroom door, her mother came in.

"I just have one question," said Mrs. Baxter. She had tried on Raven's Mama Baxter disguise, complete with fat suit, purple outfit, and hat. "When you put this on, exactly *what* mother were you thinking of?"

Raven gave her mother a sheepish look.

There really was no winning this one, she thought, but maybe one of Cory's Three Cs would do the trick.

"You look bootylicious," she said with a shrug.

Gaze into the future and take a sneak peek at the next *That's So Raven* story. . . .

Adapted by Alice Alfonsi
Based on the series created by
Michael Poryes
Susan Sherman
Based on the teleplay written
by Bob Keyes & Doug Keyes

Raven Baxter glanced around the empty gymnasium.

"Eddie?" she called, tapping her stacked black boot against the slick wood floor. *"Hello?"*

With a frown, Raven checked her watch.

Her best friend Eddie Thomas had asked her to meet him here during lunch period. Well, here she was. So where was he?

A minute later, the lights dimmed. A spotlight came on. Static crackled over the loudspeakers, and a voice echoed off the gymnasium's brick walls.

". . . And now, introducing the newest member of Bayside's basketball team. Starting Guard Eddie 'Nothin-But-Net' Thomas!"

The lights came up, and Eddie burst through the locker room doors. "Three seconds left," he called, dribbling across the court. "Thomas charges down the floor. He makes his move, drops to the rim—"

Swish! The ball greased through the net like it was covered in butter.

"Yes! Thomas wins the championship!" cried Eddie. "And the crowd goes wild!"

Not just the crowd, Raven thought with a

grin. Eddie had been practicing for months to make the cut. Now he'd done it—he'd made his dream come true.

"Congratulations, Eddie!" she squealed, her heels clicking across the gym floor. "You made the team! I'm so happy for you!"

"Thank you, thank you," said Eddie as Raven threw her arms around him. Smiling, he waited for his best friend to end her "Big Squeeze."

It was a *long* wait.

Okay, thought Eddie, there's such a thing as feeling the love *too* much. "Uh, and now the crowd *stops* hugging," he told her.

"That's right," said Raven, realizing she was doing the *girly* thing. Which was not cool, because Eddie was a *guy* friend.

Think *macho*, Raven told herself. "Woof, woof, woof!" she shouted in a deep voice, her fist pumping the air. "Home doggie, awright.

High five!" Then she slapped Eddie's hand and asked, "So, when did you find out?"

"This morning." Eddie twirled the ball on his finger. "Coach says I'm starting guard for the rest of the season. I just have to pull at least a C-plus on all my midterms."

"Oh," said Raven.

"Right on," said Eddie.

He tossed the basketball to Raven. But when she held out her hands, she caught more than just the ball. She also snagged a glimpse of the future. . . .

Through her eye
The vision runs
Flash of future
Here it comes—

I see the top of a desk.
Now I see a hand. It's holding a piece of

paper. Uh-oh, it's a test paper. Spanish class. Multiple choice.

Whoa! Looks like a packet of ketchup exploded on the page. Every single question has an angry red circle around the correct answer, which means the kid who took this test got almost every question wrong.

Now I'm seeing the name on top of the test. . . .

Oh, no. No, no, no—the name I'm seeing cannot be Eddie Thomas.

But it is . . . and now I'm seeing Eddie's face. He's looking at his grade—a big fat letter in a big red circle.

"An F?" he cries. He looks totally crushed!

When the vision ended, Raven blinked—and saw Eddie staring at her.

"What? What? What? Did you have a vision?" he asked. "Did it have anything to do with me dating a cheerleader . . . and *another* cheerleader?"

"Eddie," said Raven, "I have visions, not fantasies."

Eddie raised an eyebrow. Okay, he thought, so the cheerleader scenario was out. But he still wanted to know what Raven had seen.

Raven blinked at Eddie then swallowed nervously. "But you know," she said, chickening out, "it wasn't anything important."

Eddie sighed with relief. Then he took back the basketball and threw it in a perfect arc across the court. *Whoosh!* The ball sailed through the hoop.

"Man," Eddie said with a grin, "this is the best day of my life. Nothing can stop me now."

Nothing but a big red F on your next Spanish test, thought Raven. But she didn't dare tell him. How could she?

"Yeah, right," Raven said. "Nothing."

Get Cheetah Power!

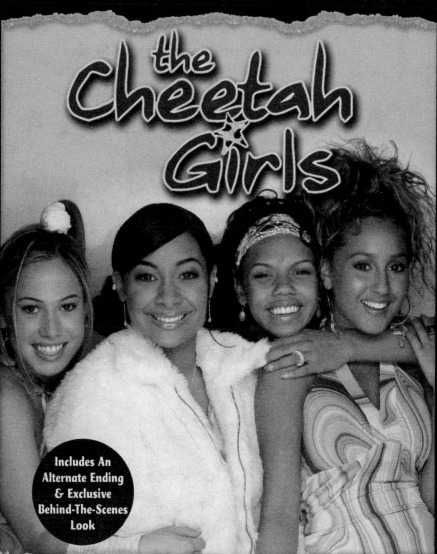

the **Cheetah Girls**

Includes An Alternate Ending & Exclusive Behind-The-Scenes Look